Can I Love Again

Can I Love Again

the heartbreak shorts, Volume 1

Dominique Thomas

Published by Dominique Thomas, 2019.

Some people are going to leave you but it's not the end of your story.
That's the end of their part in your story....

Prelude

The beat of her heart was so loud she wondered if he could hear it? She was done. Sick and tired of being alone while being with someone. Her eyes traveled his way as she watched him search the room for his wallet. It was now or never.

"I can't do this anymore," she said breaking the silence. Forcing him to pay attention to her. Something that he once gave her freely was now something she rarely received.

Times had drastically changed.

Dave snatched his keys off his dresser and frowned at his wife. He was tired and in need of a drink. Once again Bahja was looking for a reason to fight with him and he wasn't in the fucking mood for it.

"Can't do what?"

Bahja stared at Dave wondering where it all went wrong with them?

"This, us, this marriage."

Dave was shocked at her reply but didn't let it show. His pride wouldn't allow for him too.

"What are you saying Bahja? Just like that, you want a divorce?"

Bahja sighed. Did she? Could she? No words were strong enough to fall from her pouty lips. She ran a ragged hand through her chocolate strands. This was a man she'd given her all to. She'd chosen him over her family now she only had him and her sons. While she loved her kids, she was no longer happy with her husband. He was content with them merely co-existing but Bahja needed more.

She craved more.

She wanted passion. It had been a time when Dave would stare at her with so much love and adoration it would set her body ablaze. Somehow, he'd forgotten about her. She was no longer his priority and for years she ignored it, but she couldn't anymore.

"Dave, I love you. You know that. You also know how I feel about love. I've waited for years, done counseling and everything I could think of, yet you still ignore me."

Dave groaned and shook his head. He was handsome. Tall, dark and sinfully sexy. Bahja still remembered the day she'd seen him at the Underground Mall. He'd been with his boys bullshitting around while she'd been at her father's jewelry store. He owned twenty at the time which later turned into fifty.

Bahja gave Dave her heart and her body the first year while being with him. They began a relationship that was frowned upon by Bahja's family. Bahja was asked to choose and she chose Dave without having to give it a second thought.

Dave took her in, they were soon married, and three people showed up for the ceremony. While Bahja's Albanian family frowned on her union to an African American man Dave's family didn't show because he'd neglected to mention Bahja, however, once they did meet her, they let it be known that she wasn't their cup of tea. Bahja and Dave's sons ended up being turned away by both families because of the color of their skin.

Bahja sat on her bed with her eyes on Dave. She felt like he could possibly still love her, but she wasn't sure. He hadn't said or shown it in years.

"Are you in love with me?" she asked quietly.

Dave's angry eyes glared over at Bahja.

"Of course, I am. What would make you ask me some silly shit like that?"

Bahja's eyes watered.

"Because I haven't felt that love in a very long time, Dave. I want a divorce," Bahja replied.

Dave nodded. The sadness he felt from her response showed on his handsome brown face. He dropped his head and sighed deeply. When his eyes lifted and fell on her he shrugged.

"I do everything I can to please you. I don't know what else you want from me so if that's gonna make you happy then do what you have to do Bahja," he said before exiting the bedroom.

Bahja's tears were immediate. She fell back on her bed and pulled her covers up over her body. Her eyes landed on a picture of her and her husband and she could feel her chest tighten. She'd given him her everything. So much and all she wanted in return was his love. She didn't feel like she was asking for the impossible.

"He didn't even fight me on it," she mumbled with her tears clouding her vision. Bahja shook her head as she cried harder. "He didn't even fight me," she said again.

One

Are you okay? Should we come get you? We could all do something together. Maybe hookah or go shopping? Vashti was even asking about you.

A small smile covered Bahja's face at her friend's words.

Life had been hard. It hadn't always been that way, however. She'd been born to wealthy parents and lived a perfect childhood. It wasn't until she met her late husband that things took a turn for the worst. He was everything her family didn't want for her. She was young and in love and when she chose to keep a child with him, she lost her family.

Bahja was Albanian and her family frowned upon her relationship with an African American man. They simply wanted her to marry the man they had been preparing her to be with, but she didn't want that. In return, she lost them.

Bahja swallowed hard as she replied to Neveah's text.

I promise you I'm good. I love you all so much for it though. Please don't worry. I will be fine.

Bahja put her phone away and took a sip of her wine from the bottle. She sat on the bed with her eyes watery. She missed her husband. She might not have been in love with him anymore but to have him die unexpectedly and know that the last thing on his mind was her wanting a divorce hurt her. Dave was also her friend and the father of her two small sons. They no longer had him. Were too young to remember him and that was what hurt Bahja the most.

Bahja found herself homeless just months after losing Dave and was tossed out onto the street. She had no help from her family or Dave's and was sleeping in her car then finally a shelter. The shelter was where she'd met Neveah. Neveah had been a light of love in her life. She'd gone from being her friend to her family. Bahja loved Neveah and all the people that had come with her.

Neveah ran a nonprofit charity called Black Love with her fiancé's mother and Bahja worked with Neveah closely on the charity. It gave Bahja so much joy to help women and families in need. People like her.

Bahja had recently moved from Atlanta to Detroit with Neveah and was living in a beautiful home in the suburbs of OakPark. She shared the home with Neveah who was in the process of moving into a new home with her fiancé who was also there with them.

"Don't be mad. I caught them leaving out with the boys and I stopped in. I just wanted to check on you."

Micah's deep voice startled Bahja. She dropped her wine bottle on her leg and winced out in pain. He rushed over to her and picked it up as she rubbed the tender spot the glass bottle had fallen on.

"You scared the shit out of me! Micah today isn't a good day," she said frowning.

Micah nodded with his eyes on her. He sat the wine bottle on the dresser and helped her stand up. Bahja avoided eye contact with him as he pulled her into his arms.

For two years she'd been without a man. Without affection and she missed everything that came from having the opposite sex by your side. Bahja closed her eyes as Micah tenderly rubbed her back. She'd met him through Neveah and from the start he'd been intriguing to her.

He was handsome. Tall, charming and always smelled so damn good. Micah had impeccable style and lived up to his street name Pretty Boy with ease. However, it was the things that they had in common that made Bahja interested in him. Micah too had been homeless. They shared a lot of the same struggles and that made it easy for them to relate to one another.

It was Micah's not so friendly ex-girlfriend Rian that made Bahja back away from him. Bahja had unexpectedly been attacked by her and after spending hours in jail decided to walk away from the situation. She liked Micah but until he could guarantee that she didn't have to deal with that type of shit she was good on him.

"I missed your pretty lil ass," Micah expressed staring down at her.

Bahja sluggishly rubbed her face to clear her thoughts. She went over to her bed and laid down. Her head was spinning from all the wine in her system. Bahja could usually drink like a fish but had been killing bottles since she'd woken up and was now feeling it.

"Micah please," she mumbled with heavy lids.

Micah kicked off his sneakers and joined her in the bed. He pulled her into his arms and her head fell on his muscular chest. Bahja studied his handsome face as he stared back at her. Micah was the kind of man your mom warned you about. The type that looked so good you just fucking knew he would break your heart. He possessed smooth tawny brown skin with a few tattoos on his forearms but nothing major. The one tattoo that he did have that stood out the most was the heart on his chest with his mother and sisters name in it. It was extremely detailed and shaded in a way that showed off the tattoo artist's immaculate talent. Micah rocked his silky thick hair in a low cut even fade and he also had a full beard that wasn't outrageously long. He kept it groomed at all times.

The slant of his dark eyes along with the fullness of his lips always drove Bahja wild. She often lusted over him but hadn't taken it there because she did feel bad. Dave was gone and a part of her felt like it wasn't right to want someone else so soon.

"You wanna talk about him?" he asked.

Bahja smiled weakly. Micah was always so attentive to her.

"No but thank you. Let's just sleep," she murmured.

Micah began to rake his fingers through her soft strands. Bahja closed her eyes and his lips pressed against her forehead.

"It's not gone be that easy," Micah said quietly.

Bahja opened her eyes confused by his words.

"Huh?"

Micah looked down at her beautiful face and licked his lips.

"It's not gone be that easy to get rid of a nigga. I know my ex-was out of line. All that drama and shit was too much but I want this. I want you and I liked what we were building. Don't walk away from that ma. Your worth fighting for," he replied and Bahja had to close her eyes.

She hugged his body tighter as her thoughts drifted to her late husband. Micah wanted to fight for her, and it had only been months, yet Dave was willing to walk away without a fight.

"I didn't love him anymore. The last thing I said was I want a divorce. He left to go have a drink and, on his way, home he was killed in that accident. Life is so short," she said quietly.

Micah continued running his hands through her hair.

"We all living to die. I hate that happened though ma. I'm sure he would be proud of you. Proud of how far you came and how good you're doing. Focus on that. I know you a little lush and shit when you wanna be, but you bent right now ma. That's not a good look," he told her.

Bahja rolled her eyes.

"I'm not a lush. I just like a good drink. I've been drinking since I was fifteen. My grandfather used to give it to me with my dinner. In other countries teenagers can legally drink so don't worry about me," she replied. "*I mean just because I have one, maybe two drinks don't make me an alcoholic*," she repeated sounding like Eddie Kane off of the Five Heartbeats.

Micah cracked up laughing.

"Something wrong with your ass but I'm just making sure you good. Just cause you not fucking with me don't mean I'm not fucking with you. I can't stop thinking about you," he revealed to her.

Bahja looked up at him searching his eyes for the truth.

"And what about Rian?"

Micah frowned.

"This is about us. You know I'm not with her and I made it clear that I'm not fucking around. If she pops up on some crazy shit it won't be good. She's not gone force a nigga to be with her," he said getting upset.

Bahja closed her eyes again with so much on her mind it made her head hurt.

"I just don't want any drama coming my way. That won't be my life," she let him know in a tired voice.

Micah tugged on her hair gently and she gazed up at him.

"And it won't be. Just give me one more chance to make you smile. I promise you won't regret it," he said and kissed her lips.

Two

"This is cool."

Micah nodded coolly. Always so handsome and laid back with his shit. Bahja watched the women in the line stare at him as he kept his attention on her. While she wore ripped jeans with a white cami and multi-colored kimono he was the star of the show. Micah had on black jeans with a white and black collard Gucci shirt that had the g's on the collar. On his feet were a pair of Gucci sneakers while a black cap covered his head. He held her hand tightly as Bahja glanced up at him.

"What sexy?" he asked and chuckled.

Bahja smiled. Since he'd popped up at her place they been back tight and so far, drama free. She'd missed him and was happy to be in his presence.

"Nothing, simply happy to be around you. How was your trip to Dallas?"

Micah shrugged as they moved up a step in the line. Micah's eyes couldn't stop glancing at the woman in front of them and he paid her so much attention that it made Bahja look her way. The woman happened to glance back and when she spotted Micah, she quickly walked over to them.

"Hey! I was just talking with Rian the other day. What's going on?" the attractive woman asked Micah.

Micah cleared his throat and Bahja took notice of how nervous he was acting.

"Ain't shit. Gina this is Bahja, Bahja this is Rian's friend," he said introducing the two women.

Gina looked Bahja up and down and immediately rolled her eyes. She'd only come over to be messy. She had no intentions on playing nice with the hoe that ruined her friend's relationship.

"Anyway, when you gone come to your senses?" Gina asked Micah.

"Come to his senses about what exactly?" Bahja asked looking Gina's way.

Gina looked at Bahja and laughed.

"Sweetie if I fought like you, I would just keep quiet. Unless you done had some lessons."

Bahja looked Gina over and smiled at her.

"And if I looked like you sweetie I would just be fucked. What I would never want was for my girls or myself to have to beg anyone to be with me. It's rather pathetic any way you look at it. Rian knows the truth, she knows I had nothing to do with whatever happened in her relationship and at this point, I really don't care. What I won't deal with is disrespect. Clearly, your mom never took the time out to teach your ass some manners, so I'll give you some pointers. It's best to mind your own fucking business in life. Speak to people, be nice and if you're not that cute at least have a good disposition to you. Just doing little things like that can get you far," Bahja replied and wiping the smile off of Gina's face.

Micah pushed Bahja behind him as he frowned at Gina. Bahja walked away as he let Gina have it. Being around Gina and hearing her speak on the fight she'd had with Rian pissed her the fuck off. Fighting had never been her thing and she was okay with that. Bahja had never lived a life where it needed to be a necessity, so she wasn't ashamed of her lack thereof when it came to scrapping. What Bahja did know was that regardless of how good she could fight she would do it every time to protect herself.

"Hey, come here," Micah said walking up behind Bahja. His arms wrapped around her waist and instead of letting her go to the bar he took her back outside. Micah led Bahja over to the line they'd just been standing in and he grabbed her face. Bahja frowned as he peered down at her. "Don't let these bitches get to you. You know where I'm at and where I wanna be," he said before kissing her tenderly.

Micah kissed Bahja passionately as people looked on including Gina who was all in even making sure to take a picture for her friend. When Micah pulled back Bahja's lips were swollen from how hard he'd been kissing her. Micah slapped her ass and kissed her again.

"This the "D" baby. You gotta let these hoes know you not the one."

Bahja broke his gaze and looked Gina's way.

"Or you handle it so that they don't even walk up to me with the bullshit," she replied making Micah chuckle.

"And I did," he quickly added before pulling her to his side.

For hours Micah and Bahja played at the CJ Barrymore's as if they were little kids. Once they were done, they headed back to Bahja's place to chill out and have a few drinks.

"Did you have fun?" Micah asked as Bahja sat on his lap.

Bahja smiled at him as his hands did things to her ass and back that made soft moans fall between her lips.

"I did. Did you?"

Micah nodded. The weed he'd smoked had his eyes hanging low. He stood up with Bahja on his lap and laid her back on the bed. Bahja's heartbeat picked up as Micah unbuckled her pants.

"Micah…" she said quietly.

Micah shook his head as his phone began to ring.

"I just wanna taste," he said and silenced the call on his phone. Micah sat his phone on the dresser before taking off Bahja's pants. Micah then took off Bahja's black thongs and his erection became so big that Bahja could immediately see it through his jeans as it begged to be freed.

Micah's phone rang again and Bahja groaned.

"It's her," she told him.

Micah turned his phone off and pulled his shirt over his head. He then leaned down and kissed Bahja passionately on the lips while staring into her eyes.

"This is about us, baby. Let me make you feel good," he said and kissed her one last time before opening her legs.

Bahja's head fell back as Micah began to suck on her center. She hadn't felt it in so long that she nearly came the minute his tongue made contact with her.

"Oh god," she said in a shaky voice.

Bahja's cell phone began to ring repeatedly. Bahja touched the top of Micah's head and he glanced up at her. His thick lips were coated in her juices as his eyes connected with her's.

"What's wrong?" he asked and began to slowly finger her.

Bahja whimpered but before she could enjoy the moment her phone rang again. Micah grabbed it before she could, and his face fell into a frown.

"Why the fuck are you calling her phone? Matter of fact fuck all of that shit. Don't ever fucking call her Rian!" he yelled and ended the call. Micah turned off Bahja's phone and sat it on the dresser.

Bahja tried to pull her legs back and Micah held them down tightly.

"Don't. You know where I been at. You know who I want and that's why the fuck she so mad. I promise you she will never call your shit again. I'll handle it. Okay?" he asked and added two fingers to Bahja's snug opening.

Bahja shook her head. She wasn't for the drama. She had so many questions and with every turn of Micah's fingers, she slowly forgot them. She closed her eyes as her body began to quiver. She was going to cum.

It was right fucking there.

Micah knew it as well. He leaned down and with the tip of his tongue flicked it rapidly against Bahja's clitoris. Bahja fisted the comforter and within seconds was releasing all over his fingers.

***

"Thank you for coming. Any woman that was good enough to grab my brother's attention is somebody I *have to know*," Amor said with a smile.

Bahja stopped sifting through the clothes at Mickey's Rack to look at Amor. Micah had begged her to go shopping with his sister. Amor was a good college girl that Micah said was about her business. So far Bahja was enjoying her time with the young beautiful Amor that was even more attractive than her handsome older brother.

"Well, Micah isn't someone you can ignore. I'm sure he told you about Rian."

Amor nodded while frowning.

"And I never liked that bitch! Micah bends over backward for her and she kicks him in it every time. When he told me he'd finally put her out I swear I could have cried. Micah's special," Amor stopped talking and swallowed hard. Like Micah, she remembered the hard times her family had. To Amor, Micah was not only her big brother but the father figure she so desperately needed. So, at times she felt bad for all of the things she was hiding from him. She simply knew that once he found out he would be ready to kill her.

"I heard and I'm still in shock. Rian does have a habit of playing with Micah's emotions, but she isn't violent. I think it was everything combined that made her react that way. Please don't use that against my brother though. He isn't a bad guy," Amor replied running to Micah's defense.

Bahja took in everything Amor said but still wasn't so sure if it was all worth it. Micah had kept his word and Rian hadn't called Bahja again. However, Bahja was curious to know how she'd gotten her number in the first place and Micah had told her that Rian was simply crazy.

"I know he isn't but the whole situation seems messy to me. I'm not used to that."

Amor smiled. She could tell that Bahja was cut from a different cloth.

"Are you rich?" she asked but not in a condescending way.

Bahja quickly shook her head.

"My parents are but I'm not. What made you ask me that?"

Amor shrugged. Bahja's wavy hair held a sleek shine to it. Her nails and toenails were done and while she wore plain jeans with a cream strapless bodysuit, she still screamed money.

"No disrespect. I wasn't trying to be funny. I just get that vibe from you. You have so much class. I love that, and you seem sweet. I guess only time will tell if that's true."

Bahja looked at Amor and they both laughed.

"And your brother made you out to be the Virgin Mary but like you said only time will tell how true that is," Bahja retorted smiling at Amor.

Amor laughed harder and Bahja mistakenly backed into someone. She stumbled over her heels and he caught her at the waist. His alluring cologne teased her senses as he spun her around. Bahja stared up into the handsome man's dark-skinned face and lost all train of thought. She'd run into him at her home months prior because he knew her friend Neveah's fiancé. Back then she'd been caught off guard by his good looks. As he stood before her wearing black and red while sporting a cocky smirk, she realized that it hadn't been her imagination.

Jigga was fine as fuck and the way her body came alive at the sight of him was startling.

"Look at fate. Sometimes she can ruin a niggas day or bring him a blessing. How you doing shorty, remember me?" he asked in his usual deep tone.

Bahja took a step back and Amor smacked her lips.

"I thought you said you were going to Cali for the weekend? What the fuck are you doing at the mall? You back cheating nigga!" Amor said loudly making Bahja and Jigga turn her way.

Bahja noticed that Amor was arguing with the man that was a few feet away from Jigga. The man was handsome as well but looked much older than her.

"I didn't tell you shit like that. Calm down with all that rowdy shit," Zayne told Amor.

Amor stared him up and down angrily before reaching up and slapping the taste out of his mouth. Bahja's jaw fell as Jigga rushed over and grabbed his cousin. He whispered something in his ear as Amor grabbed a nearby hanger and began to hit Zayne in the face with it.

"I knew your ass was back cheating! I'm pregnant with your damn kid and this is how you do me, nigga!" she yelled angrily.

Bahja quickly grabbed Amor and pulled her out of the store. They went to Amor's Range Rover and got in. Bahja stared at Amor not sure what to say and Amor laughed nervously. She smoothed down her honey blonde extensions and exhaled. Her heart was racing, and she was still mad as hell at her so-called man.

"I don't usually behave that way. I promise you I'm not ghetto," she said smiling at Bahja. When Bahja didn't crack a smile Amor's eyes watered. She dropped her head while breathing hard. "All my life my brother has been telling me about how I should be treated. How a good man was on his way to me and for a while I believed him. I believed that I could find someone like him until reality set in. The men I want. The fly ass niggas with the money, good looks, and big dicks aren't easily attainable. They're not Prince Charming. They aren't loyal, and they give no fucks about breaking your heart. After getting fucked over by this punk ass college boy I met Zayne. He was at his brother's dispensary and I immediately fell for him. He was so fine and was saying all of the right things. He helped me out with my school work and even waited half a year to have sex with me. We always use condoms but one of them broke and I recently discovered I was pregnant. I'm ten weeks and when I found out it was like the mask was lifted. Bahja he's a whore. He would fuck you if we let him. I hate I ever fell for his bitch ass! And he lied about his age. Like what grown ass man lies about their age? *Zayne's* bitch ass that's who. Shit, he actually lied about his name too but let his real name slip up one night while we were drunk as hell. Please don't tell Micah. He's so proud of me for staying in college and I know this will crush him."

Bahja sighed in frustration. She'd only intended to do some shopping not get placed in the middle of Amor's bullshit. Bahja rubbed Amor's arm and smiled at her.

"People will only do to them what you allow. Be it a man or a woman. To get more you have to demand it. If your baby isn't here yet and already, he's showing his ass, then that should tell you all you need to know about him. I'm not saying get an abortion, but you need to look out for Amor. No matter what don't drop out of school. A man can break your heart but don't let him ruin your life. Get your degree so no matter what you can provide for you and your child. Trust me it's the worst feeling in the world to not be able to do that," Bahja replied thinking of her own situation and how badly she struggled when Dave was killed.

"Thank you for that," Amor replied and hugged Bahja.

***

"How was the mall?"

Bahja watched Micah cut her youngest son Benji's hair. She hated keeping secrets from him but also didn't feel right telling business that wasn't her's.

"It was...*eventful*," Bahja replied with flashes of her time with Amor replaying in her mind. She also thought back on running into Jigga and her cheeks darkened. Bahja cleared her throat and glanced Micah's way. "Your sister is really beautiful and sweet."

Micah stopped cutting Benji's hair to peer up at her. His hooded eyes stared at her intently as he stood in her bathroom as if he belonged there. As if it was his home. He'd made it clear that he wanted a wife and a family. Bahja wasn't sure if she was ready for marriage again but she did feel blessed to have a man in her life that was looking for what she already had.

"You sure? You sound funny?" he asked.

Bahja smiled at him as her phone rung from the bedroom.

"Yes, I'm sure. We had fun and I'm going out with her this weekend."

Micah began to cut her sons hair again.

"Oh yeah? Where y'all going?"

Bahja noticed how sexy he was looking in his black basketball shorts with his white beater and she licked her lips.

"To some club in Royal Oak," she replied and walked away.

"She might be a bad influence on you!" he yelled.

Bahja laughed.

"If you only knew," she mumbled. She went into her bedroom and grabbed her cell off the dresser. She had several missed calls from her mother. She hadn't spoken with her mom in a year. Was shocked that she still knew her number. Her breathing picked up as she called her back.

"Honey, how are you?" her mom asked immediately answering the call.

Bahja cleared her throat.

"What do you want?" she asked in a tone that was everything but friendly.

"It's your father. He was in a bad car accident, but he survived! He's okay it's just he's different now. He says that we should speak to you. Check on you and the boys," her mom replied.

Bahja's emotions bubbled over and her tears fell. For years she wished to hear those words from her mom. However, as she stood in her bedroom, they did nothing for her. She ended the call and placed her mom on the block list along with her father's number.

"You good?" Micah asked walking up behind her.

Bahja quickly wiped her face and nodded. She put her phone away and he pulled her into his arms. Bahja sighed as he hugged her tightly.

"The kids hungry. I thought we could hit up Flemings and get you that steak you been wanting," he said to her.

Bahja smiled. She had to admit to herself that it did feel good to have him back around.

"I would love that. How was your day? I know you said you were looking to buy that strip mall."

Micah let her go and looked her up and down in a way that set her body on fire. He gently touched her hips and gave it a light squeeze. Bahja was wearing the fuck out of some jeans and he was finding it hard to keep his eyes off her.

"Yeah, shit is moving good. Hopefully, I can have it soon, so we can get that motherfucker up and running. I'm good now that I'm with you. Can I stay the night?"

Bahja nervously glanced around the room. She didn't mind him staying over when her sons were gone but with them being back, she wasn't so sure.

Micah saw the look of uncertainty on Bahja's face and pulled her back into his arms. His hard body pressed against her's as he gazed down into her eyes.

"I know the kids here. I'll be on my best behavior. Maybe just rub it a few times. Make you feel good and shit," he said lowly.

Bahja's cheeks darkened and she slowly nodded. Micah slapped her ass while smiling.

"Bet let me go wash up," he said and walked away.

Bahja washed up her son's in the bathroom across from their bedroom and changed them into clean clothes. She then turned on their favorite cartoon movie and quickly changed into some black jeans with a white lace off the shoulders top. Bahja put mousse in her hair to wave it up and applied powder to her face and sheer gloss to her full lips. She sat with her sons once she was done and watched them while smiling as she thought of how lucky she was to have them.

"Mommy missed you two," she said and they both smiled at her before turning back to their movie.

"Emory's mom is so mad your taking them to the daycare full-time. She loves them so much already," Neveah said peaking her head into the big bedroom.

Bahja smiled at her. Neveah was carrying her pregnancy well and it showed with the beautiful glow on her face.

"I know she does. I just wanted to make it easy on all of us. I love how you all have taken us in, but it isn't her job to watch my sons. I can afford daycare now. *Thank God.*"

"Aye its, not about that. We family and my mom love them little dudes," Emory, Neveah's fiancé said walking up.

Bahja smiled at him and watched as Neveah gave him a lusty gaze.

"Well we're about to go watch Martin and lay down," Neveah said and damn near dragged Emory away from the door.

Bahja laughed.

"That's why your ass is pregnant now!" she yelled messing with her friend.

Neveah had gone through hell and back with Emory. Their story was unconventional, but it was theirs. Bahja was happy that they had made it to the other side.

"Y'all ready?" Micah asked walking up.

Bahja's sons jumped up at the sound of his voice and rushed to his side. Bahja watched him play with them before turning his attention to her. Micah wore all black with a Detroit fitted sitting on his head. Around his neck was a Cuban link chain and on his wrist was a Breitling covered in diamonds. He was clean like always and Bahja prayed she was making the right decisions. She saw the happiness in her sons' eyes whenever they looked Micah's way. She didn't wanna let them or herself down.

"Yes, let's go," she said and stood up.

Bahja walked over to them and Micah slapped her ass when she moved passed him. They left the house and got into Micah's Range Rover.

Micah took Bahja and her sons to Flemings in Livonia. After waiting for twenty minutes they were seated. They quickly ordered their food and while the boys played with each other. Bahja sat next to her oldest son while Micah sat beside her youngest son who was in a highchair. Micah smirked at Bahja as he peeped a few niggas looking her way. No matter where they went Bahja was always the center of attention.

"You looking beautiful like always ma. You working tomorrow?"

Bahja blushed. It felt so domestic to be with him and her sons in the restaurant. She nodded and smiled.

"I am, and I also decided to sign up for school. It's something I always wanted to pursue but I held it off for their dad. I let him chase his dream and I chose to stay at home with the kids. It's never too late to go back, though right?"

Micah licked his lips. He sat up and leaned across the table. His strong hand brushed against her's lovingly.

"Nah it's never too late for that. I'm proud of you. What you going back for?"

Bahja's eyes connected with Jigga's and she squirmed in her seat. She quickly brought her attention to Micah but the look he gave her was cold. He removed his hand and glanced across the room. He spotted Jigga and some nigga he didn't know sitting down with two beautiful women at their table and he chuckled. Micah looked back at Bahja and noticed she was staring down at her phone.

He knew they weren't exclusive still the idea of her entertaining anyone besides him pissed him off.

"You wanna go speak to him?" Micah asked with a slight attitude.

Bahja smiled as she set her phone down. She sipped her wine and relaxed as the cool liquid slid down her throat.

"Micah don't but I wanna go to school for journalism. I would love to start my own mommy magazine. For women that don't have it all together. I think that would be nice," she replied.

Micah stood up and went around to her side of the table. He leaned down and kissed her cheek. Bahja could feel the butterflies fluttering in her stomach as he caressed her neck.

"Anything you do will be amazing. I believe in you ma," he whispered and sealed his words with a kiss.

Micah went back to his seat and as he sat down Bahja's eyes inadvertently connected with Jigga's. He shook his head before turning his attention back to his people. Bahja looked back at Micah and was relieved when she saw he was answering a text on his phone. Bahja's phone vibrated on the table and she picked it up. Her stomach knotted up when she saw she had a message from an unknown number.

I'm trying to not step on that nigga's toes, but you can't be staring at me looking so fucking beautiful and not expect me to wanna come take you away. Don't ask how I got your number, instead ask yourself if you gonna use mine? It's not a coincidence that we keep seeing each other shorty.

"You good?" Micah asked Bahja making her jump.

She quickly exited Jigga's text and looked at him. Micah was attractive, and she did feel a strong connection with him. Juggling men had never been her thing, so she chose to ignore Jigga. She blocked his number and put her phone away. She smiled at Micah and he relaxed in his seat.

"Yes, just ready to eat and go home," she replied.

Micah chuckled.

"Shit me and you both baby," he replied and Bahja made a real effort to not look Jigga's way for the rest of the night.

She wanted Micah to have all her attention.

Three

"I see Micah pretty much spends his nights with us now. Which is a good thing because Emory and I found a house. We actually closed on it the other day. It's gorgeous Bahja!" Neveah said excitedly.

Bahja smiled and hugged her friend. They were inside of the offices of the Black Love Charity that Neveah ran and closing up for the night. After preparing for their first fundraiser they were both beat and ready to head home.

"I'm so happy for you! Where is it at?"

Neveah went over to her desk and grabbed her purse. She'd gained quite a few pounds, but it suited her well. Neveah and Emory had learned a month prior that she was carrying twin girls and weren't as surprised as everyone else. When Bahja asked her why she wasn't shocked, Neveah simply said her love angel had given them a heads up.

"I believe he said it's in Northville. Its huge and I wish you and the boys were coming with us," she replied with a pout.

Bahja waved Neveah off. She pulled out a shot from her tote bag and Neveah rolled her eyes.

"And I'm pissed that you get to drink, and I don't. I'm happy to be carrying these kids but it's like my life is being put on hold for months because of this. I keep telling Emory that wine won't hurt the babies. Hell, people smoke crack and their kids come out fine. I'm sure some red wine won't cause any damage," Neveah joked.

Bahja laughed and tossed back her drink. She threw away the empty bottle and looked at her friend.

"For your babies, you have to be at one hundred percent. Going eight or nine months without liquor is worth the health of your child. You'll get used to it and when you hear the babies cry in that hospital room, you'll know that it was all worth it. I love my liquor now but with both of my kids, I was a health nut. It's women wishing they could have kids, wishing they could experience what you're feeling right now. You and Emory are being blessed with two little princesses. That's so special Neveah. Don't take that for granted," Bahja told her.

Neveah sighed while rubbing her belly.

"I won't. I swear you always know the right things to say. Are you and Pretty Boy a couple now? And did you fuck him last night?"

Bahja fell into her seat and twirled it in a circle. She'd tossed back two shots and was feeling good. She wasn't drunk but had a nice buzz which was what she was aiming for.

"Neveah, I have a confession."

Neveah went over to her and sat on the edge of her desk.

"I'm all ears. Was it that bad?"

Bahja rolled her eyes.

"I kind of thought of Jigga while he was eating me out. I know it's wrong, but I couldn't help it! He's like always on my damn mind."

Neveah's hand shot to her mouth. She grinned at Bahja before they both started laughing.

"I'm not surprised. Jigga is that nigga. Every time he comes around, I just stare down at the ground. It's like if I even take a chance and look at him my nipples might get hard. Plus, it doesn't help that Emory be watching my ass like a hawk and shit. But Pretty Boy is fine too. I thought you were falling for him."

Bahja shrugged. She was, then the drama with his ex-happened and she found herself getting turned off from him.

"I was but something changed. It was Rian and her bullshit."

Neveah stood up and rubbed her steadily growing belly.

"Or Jigga and his big ass imprint. You don't have a ring on your finger, so you should date them both. Hell, men do it all the time. You need to know for sure who you want. Play the field before you make any huge decisions," Neveah advised her.

Bahja stared up at her.

"But what if Micah gets mad? I'm not trying to hurt him."

Neveah nodded.

"You're a good honest person. You also can't help how you feel. Put Bahja first not Micah. Shit if he wanted to be back with Rian, I promise you that's where his ass would be. Don't let him bully you into being with him. Be with him because he's the only man that makes you feel good on the inside. Not because he was the first Detroit nigga that you met. I would take my time if it was me."

Bahja wished that it was that simple. After leaving work Bahja grabbed her sons from daycare, fed and bathed them before taking a hot shower. She finally climbed into bed and Micah called her. She knew that he was itching to come over, but she wasn't particularly in the mood to see him. For the last week, he'd been stuck to her like glue and she was relieved to have a break from him.

Bahja yawned as she scrolled down to Jigga's name. She unblocked him and called his phone. She closed her eyes as she listened to the line ring. Bahja also couldn't ignore the way her heart thumped wildly in her chest at the thought of talking with him.

"I hit big at MGM then you hitting my line. It's gotta be my lucky night. How you been?" he asked answering the call.

Bahja exhaled. His voice just did something to her.

"I've been good. I'm tired," she replied with her eyes still closed.

"Damn you sound like it. Wish I could come over and rock your sexy ass to sleep. Do you have a job?"

Bahja laughed lightly.

"Yes, do you?"

It was Jigga's turn to chuckle.

"Something like that. Can I bring you breakfast to your job tomorrow?"

Bahja cleared her throat. She thought of Micah and felt guilty for even talking with Jigga on the phone.

"I don't know. I am seeing someone."

Jigga laughed again.

"But you wanna be seeing me. We both grown as fuck beautiful. You don't have to sugar coat it. You feel the same shit that I do, and you interested in me. Shit I know I'm feeling the fuck out of you. I'm not into begging or pleading though sexy. That's never been my style. How about when you're looking to see me face to face by yourself you hit me up? How that sound?" he asked.

Bahja smiled.

"I like the sound of that," she said quietly.

Jigga sighed.

"And I like the sound of your voice. Got me wondering how you sound when other shit's being done to you. You have a good night beautiful. Just don't waste too much more time. I'm itching to have you. You like the next big drug and shit. I keep talking about you to my people. Dreaming about your ass and shit. Its real out here," he said making them both laugh.

Bahja's line clicked with Micah and she exhaled.

"Well I'll let you go," she told Jigga and clicked over. "Hey, you," she said talking to Micah.

Micah sucked his teeth.

"I won't go from one fucked up situation to the other. All I ask is that you keep it real with me baby," he replied.

Bahja sat up in the bed while frowning.

"Where did that come from?"

"I'm not stupid ma. Can you open the door for me?" he asked.

Bahja raised her brows.

"So, you just gone pop up at my home? It's like that?" she asked getting out of the bed.

Micah chuckled.

"I'm serious about you. Maybe you don't feel the same way and if that's the case let a nigga know. You wanna fuck with somebody else Bahja? Do you?" he asked.

Bahja's heart beat faster. Did she? Jigga was sexy, fine, handsome, anything in the category of looking good that you could name but what else did she know about him? She was actually building something with Micah and wasn't ready to let that go. She left out of her bedroom and walked down the stairs. Bahja ended the call and opened her front door. Micah stood on the other end holding a little blue Tiffany's bag along with some of her favorite wine and a to-go bag filled with her favorite seafood. Bahja's stomach growled at the smells wafting her way.

"You never answered my question," Micah said stepping into the house.

Bahja stepped back and gave him a quick once-over. Micah was wearing navy jeans with a white tee that had a white and red Pistons jersey tossed over it. He was sporting a fresh haircut and smelling better than the food. She watched him step out of his shoes and look her way. Micah always stared at her like it was his first time seeing her.

"You look tired," he said noticing her red eyes.

Bahja stood before him in a two-piece pajama pants set with her hair in two loose braids. She walked up to him and hugged his side. He seemed upset with her and the last thing she was trying to do was hurt him.

"I am. Did you miss me?" she asked him.

Micah chuckled. He grabbed her ass with his free hand and cuffed it in a way that made her cream her thongs.

"Yeah but you ain't miss me. Dodging a nigga's calls and shit. I see what time it is. If you wanna fuck with these other niggas out here just let me know Bahja," he said letting her go.

Bahja walked away and he stared down at her ample ass as he followed her up the stairs. They went into Bahja's bedroom and he stripped out of his clothes. Bahja climbed into her bed and waited on him. Micah went to the opposite side and sat down. He began to eat and the longer he ate the seafood without offering her any the angrier she became. Bahja started to breathe heavily and Micah fell out laughing.

"You not eating shit with me. You didn't even want me to come over," he said turning to her.

Bahja acted like she was about to hug him, and she grabbed his tray. She hungrily tore into the food as her cell phone started to ring. Micah grabbed the phone because it was on the nightstand beside him and he looked at the screen. He'd upgraded her to the iPhone X a month prior and it was trivial but still worked his nerves that she had niggas calling on a phone he'd paid for.

"Here you go," he said tossing the phone to her. He'd taken the liberty of picking up the call.

Bahja stopped eating her shrimp to look down at her phone. Jigga's name was displayed on the screen but the call had ended. Bahja tried to grab the phone and Micah quickly picked it up. Angrily he looked at her as he stood up.

"What's the deal with you and this nigga? You need to be telling me about that shit right now or I'm gone," he told her.

Bahja sat the tray down on her nightstand. She stood up and went over to Micah. She touched his chest and he backed up. Micah shook his head as he passed her the phone.

The only reason he was keeping his composure was because her sons were home. He wasn't trying to scare the kids.

"What the fuck is up?" he asked again.

Bahja fiddled with her shiny black phone.

"We talked once on the phone," she replied nervously.

Micah swallowed hard.

"And."

Bahja shrugged. She looked at Micah as he stood in front of her in his red Ethika boxers with his sexy body on display. Her eyes couldn't help but fall on his imprint. He might have been upset with her, but his dick wasn't as it begged to be freed from the pricey boxers.

"Bahja what else," Micah asked noticing her staring at his dick. He chuckled as he stared her way. "You just looking for any nigga to make you smile, is that it? Cause if that's the case then I can leave. You beautiful as fuck, of course, you got options but don't get this shit confused ma. A nigga not hard up for no bitch. I got options too but I'm choosing to be here with you. If you confused on who you wanna fuck with then I'll make the decision for you. I ain't got time for these fucking games," he said and went over to his clothes.

Bahja felt like shit as she watched him toss on his clothes. She went over to him and grabbed his face. Micah tried to pull back and she stood on the tip of her toes to kiss him.

"It's you and I'm sorry. I wanna build something with you," she whispered against his lips before kissing him again.

Micah took a few minutes to give in but when he did Bahja found herself on her back naked with her legs wrapped around his waist. His thick mushroom shaped head poked at her opening before he gently pushed in. Bahja moaned and her back arched up off the bed.

Micah grunted and closed his eyes. His heart raced as he felt his dick being hugged by Bahja's wet walls. She was tight as fuck.

"Damn you tight," he said and slowly started to move.

Bahja whimpered. Her body hadn't felt that type of pleasure in way too long. She opened her legs wider and Micah looked down into her eyes. The way she felt was unbelievable. Velvety soft with a snug grip and he was in pure bliss from being inside of her.

No condoms stood between them and he was able to feel all of her essence.

"You feel so good. This dick doing its job Bahja?" he asked fucking her harder.

Bahja nodded weakly. Her body was starting to shake all over. Micah felt her walls contract around him and he smirked at her.

"Yeah, it is. Relax and cum all over me," he coached pushing her legs back further.

Bahja cried and Micah began to kiss her as he fucked her so hard that he was pushing her up the bed. Between her climaxing, his girth and stroke Bahja was in heaven. Her eyes leaked with tears of joy as he finally released on her belly. Micah breathed hard as he gazed down at her.

"Block that nigga from calling you," he told her with his heart pumping wildly in his chest.

Bahja weakly nodded.

"It's already done" she whispered, and he licked his lips.

"That's what I like to hear. Let's take this shit to the shower," he said and picked her up. Micah tossed her over his shoulder and carried her away as her limp body clung onto him for dear life.

Four

"I can't believe I'm doing this," Amor said wiping her eyes.

Bahja rubbed her leg. She was a woman and she wouldn't judge.

"You're doing what you have to do. It's only if you agree, however. Do you really wanna have this abortion?" she asked her.

Amor nodded with her eyes closed. Zayne had disappeared on her. Only then did she realize how much she didn't know about him. Besides his brother's business, she had no other way to get in contact with him. All she wanted was support and he refused to give her that.

"He's a fuck nigga I swear. I asked him could we co-parent and he sent me back the eye emojis. After that, his ass has been missing in action. His brother is always nice when I see him, but I can tell even he's getting tired of my pop-ups. I refuse to bring a kid into this toxic ass situation. I can't, and I won't. I pray God forgives me for this. I feel really bad. I do," Amor replied sadly before leaning on Bahja.

Bahja rubbed Amor's arm feeling bad for her as well until the urge to turn around became so great that she had to see what was trying to get ahold of her attention. Sitting in the doctor's office was none other than Rian. Her eyes connected with Bahja's and instead of coming off angry she looked scared.

Amor looked up with Bahja and frowned when she spotted her brother's ex-girlfriend. Amor's eyes fell on Rian's stomach and she jumped up from her seat.

"Are you really about to sneak and kill his baby? Wow, how fucking cruel can you be?" Amor asked and pulled out her phone.

A few people glanced their way as Bahja stared down at Rian's very round stomach. Bahja gathered she had to be right at the limit to get an abortion.

"Amor don't! This has nothing to do with your little-spoiled ass," Rian said coming over to them.

Amor walked away and Bahja ran a rough hand through her hair. It was always fucking something with Micah. It never failed. She started to count up the weeks in her head and Rian sat beside her.

"It's his. He came over one night to tell me to leave you alone and it happened. We were both drunk, I was hurt, and he was honestly fucked up. He probably doesn't even remember it, but I do. I don't care why you or Amor is here. All I care about is handling my business. I won't bring a kid into my broken relationship," Rian said sounding defeated with the situation.

"My brother is on his way, Rian. He said that if you go through with this, he's fucking you up," Amor said coming back into the room.

"Miss you all will have to leave. This is a private facility," the nurse said walking over with a doctor.

Rian stood up with Bahja and she glared at Amor.

"You little bitch. I should slap some sense into your dumb ass. He can't force me to have this kid and just why are you here?"

Amor grabbed her bag and glared at Rian.

"To get a check-up hoe," she lied and pulled Bahja away.

Bahja, Amor, and Rian walked out of the clinic and found Micah pulling into the parking lot damn near on two wheels. Bahja stood back quietly as she watched him jump out of his Range Rover and walk over to them angrily. Micah looked down at Rian's big bump and shook his head. The anger that covered his face was enough for all of the women to stay quiet. Neither of them wanted to make him angrier.

"I can't believe you would even take your big ass up in there to try and have that shit! That's fucking murder. What the fuck is wrong with you!" he yelled making Rian jump.

Rian began to cry and the whole scene was all too much for Bahja. She walked away, and Amor followed her. They quickly got into Amor's car and Amor pulled off. Bahja glanced over at Amor and cleared her throat.

"I like you, Amor. Your immature but that's to be expected. You're young and with age comes wisdom. What you did today wasn't right. You were just asking me to not judge you and the first thing you do is call your brother when you see Rian. She had a right to make her own decision as well. Granted I wouldn't have gone if I was that big but who are we to judge her? Just take me home," Bahja said tired of the bullshit.

Amor shook her head.

"Micah is my everything. All he ever wanted was kids and I wasn't about to let her get over on him again. My brother adores the ground you walk on. Even with that baby, he will still want you so don't be worried about that," Amor replied wanting to reassure her of Micah's love for her.

Bahja laughed lightly. She pulled a small wine bottle from her bag and popped the cap on it. She glanced over at Amor and realized that she had a whole lot to learn about life.

"Amor I wasn't worried about that. Even you can see that a baby won't keep a man so that was the furthest thing from my mind. We have to treat people how we want to be treated. I can't stand Rian. I met her and immediately I let her know about your brother and whatever it was we had going on because I didn't want drama. I didn't come into that situation as a mistress. When he came to Atlanta, he told me they weren't together. Still, she showed her ass, attacked me and everything. Since then she's been a fucking nightmare to deal with. I get it they have years under their belt but that's on them not me. Even with all of that being said calling your brother never entered my mind. It wasn't our business to tell. You up there about to get rid of your baby yet you tell on her. That was foul so just take me home," she repeated getting irritated with the situation.

Amor rolled her eyes while sucking her teeth.

"That I can do," she replied and quickly took Bahja home.

Bahja walked into her place with a frown on her face. Neveah was gone with Emory to Atlanta for the weekend to see her parents and the boys were still in daycare. Bahja didn't have to get them for at least four more hours so she decided to take a quick shower.

She made herself some chicken salad and instead of laying down got on her laptop. She bought a website and after watching a few tutorials began to build her mommy blog. It wasn't a magazine, but it was a step in the right direction. And within the comfort of her own home, New Age Mommy was born. It was a blog about anything pertaining to motherhood.

Bahja had to step away from her website to pick up her sons and cook dinner for them. Micah walked into her home with Neveah and Emory hours later when the boys were asleep and Bahja was slightly peeved. She understood that he was family with them but still that was her place of peace. He didn't have the right to just walk up in her shit like he was paying something on the bills.

"You wasn't picking up your phone. We were worried ma," Micah said stepping into the living room.

Bahja closed her laptop and peered up at him. Micah had on workout gear with a black Detroit fitted. She watched Neveah stare at them questioningly as Emory hugged her from the back.

"*He* was worried. I figured you were sleep. Are you gonna come to see the house with me in the morning?" Neveah asked.

Bahja nodded while still staring at Micah. It was the way his eyes bored into her that made her nervous. The situation with Rian made her very uneasy.

"Sure," Bahja mumbled and Neveah and Emory walked away.

Micah came over to Bahja bringing with him the strong stench of weed. He leaned down and kissed her cheek.

"Come take a shower with me," he whispered. He grabbed her hand before she could respond and took her upstairs. While Micah undressed Bahja made sure her sons were still sound asleep in their bedroom. She joined Micah in the bathroom and silently took off her clothes. He turned on the water and led Bahja into the large shower.

Bahja grabbed the loofah and Micah took it from her. He pulled her to his hard, tattooed body and she gazed up at him.

Bahja felt such conflicting feelings as she looked up into his eyes.

"It's your baby?"

Micah swallowed hard.

"I slipped up once when I went to check her about fucking with you. We weren't committed to each other at the time but still, I'm sorry."

Bahja looked away from him and his strong hands grabbed her face. They slid down her body to her hips and effortlessly he picked her up. His dick seemed to immediately know where to go as it started to poke at her opening. He tried to push in and Bahja shook her head.

"Micah no," she protested. "You're running back to her unprotected then coming over here. Put me down."

Micah kissed her neck. The last thing he wanted to do was put her down.

"I'm sorry and it was only that one time. That's not where I wanna be," he whispered while teasing her opening with his head. "This changes nothing baby," Micah promised and slowly slid inside of Bahja. Bahja closed her eyes as he filled up her tight walls. "Damn baby, you wet," he said and groaned.

Bahja whimpered, and Micah tossed her legs into the crooks of his arms. He pressed her against the shower wall and Bahja cried out. He was so deep she felt like it would split her in half.

"Baby don't let this run you away," Micah said and groaned. Bahja's wetness was driving him delirious.

Bahja kept her eyes closed not wanting to see his face and it wasn't long before they were both falling apart inside of the steamy shower.

***

"This place is huge! I'm so happy for you two," Vashti said looking around.

Vashti was Neveah's fiancé sister. Neveah beamed with pride as she showed Bahja and Vashti around her five-bedroom home. She took them into the master bedroom that was halfway furnished and over to her closet. It was the real definition of a walk-in closet. It housed separate sections, a sitting area along with a vanity and makeup corner. Bahja looked around at all of the boxes and shoes that needed to be put up and shook her head.

"This is just so beautiful. I'm so happy for you!" she told her for the millionth time.

Neveah smiled but it didn't quite reach her eyes. She shifted from one foot to the other as she stared at Bahja.

"I heard Micah telling Emory that Rian was pregnant. What the fuck is that shit about?"

"She's what?" Vashti asked shocked by Neveah's revelation.

Rian was once a stylist at her salon and a friend of her's until Rian learned about Micah moving on with Bahja.

Bahja sat down in the chair at Neveah's vanity and dropped her head. All night she'd tossed and turned as Micah rested beside her. He'd placed his phone on vibrate but it hadn't stopped it from ringing all night long. Micah never picked up but Bahja was certain it was Rian blowing him up.

Bahja looked up at Neveah and Vashti with watery eyes. She wasn't necessarily crying over Micah. It was the situation in a whole that had her drained.

Already.

"Bahja," Neveah said and Bahja shook her head while holding her hand up.

"Long story short I ran into Rian yesterday. I won't say where I was because it's not my business to tell just know she was very pregnant. She was about to get an abortion and Micah was notified of that. Not by me. He shows up acting a fool on her and I leave. He told me last night after popping up with you guys that it's still about me and him.

How he is invested in making things work with me. How it was only one time. *Blah blah blah*. He said Rian is twenty-four weeks pregnant with his son. I honestly don't know how to feel. All I can think about is how ignorant she was before. I don't wanna deal with her but then I feel guilty for feeling that way because he's so good with my kids. I'm confused on what to do guys," she revealed.

Vashti found a seat on one of the ottomans in the room and Neveah sat beside her on the floor. Neveah rubbed her belly as they stared Bahja's way.

"That's bullshit! Why leave her if you're gonna go back and fuck her! Hell, you were attacked by this girl and spent the night in jail and his way of handling that was to put his dick in her?" Neveah asked.

Bahja shrugged.

"I don't know. He never said which time it was. All I know is that she's pregnant and now I feel like I need to run for the fucking hills. Then I look into his eyes and I wonder if cutting him off is the right thing to do. Micah makes me happy. He's good to my sons."

Vashti nodded smiling at her.

"And you like that feeling that he provides right?" she asked.

Bahja smiled. She thought of the security that came over her whenever he was near.

"I do," she admitted quietly.

Neveah looked her way.

"But it's nothing another man can't give you. I like Micah too. We all see how he cares about you but aren't you at least curious to know if this baby will push him back to Rian?" Neveah asked her.

Bahja looked at her friends and shrugged.

"If that's the case then he never really was mine anyway. But besides him, I started a blog. I signed up for school in the fall and I'm taking some journalism classes. It's my goal to have my own mom magazine," Bahja said changing the whole tone of the room.

Vashti and Neveah grinned at her words.

"What! I love it! Bahja yes," Neveah said and kicked her leg playfully.

Bahja laughed.

"Listen I would have jumped up, but you know I picked up some weight. I can't just be hopping up like I used to. Probably pass out or some shit," Neveah joked, and they all laughed.

"No but seriously, we're both proud of you and you have our support with anything. You can even throw your website launch party at the salon. We're so happy for you!" Vashti said standing up. She hugged Bahja and Bahja smiled at her two friends lovingly.

She'd gone years without the love from her immediate family and God had found a way to still placed people in her life that loved and cared for her. She was incredibly grateful for them.

"I love you all too. We need another church date in the near future," she told them.

Neveah nodded while smiling and Vashti stared their way.

"Just without the fighting!" she blurted out making Neveah and Bahja start laughing again.

The one time they'd gone to church together they'd ended the day in jail after fighting with Rian. It had been a day that Bahja would forever remember.

Hours later Bahja sat outside of the shelter in downtown Detroit. She'd spent two hours passing out food and helping clean up. Being around people in need and helping them was still a passion of her's. Never would she forget the days when she couldn't feed her kids let alone herself.

"Look at you," Jigga said taking a seat beside Bahja.

Bahja stopped staring at the street and glanced his way. She'd once again hit him up and like before he talked to her with no problem. She'd called Micah a few times and all of her calls had gone unanswered.

"I shouldn't have called you," Bahja said admiring Jigga's masculine beauty.

His dark skin had a natural shine to it. The black jeans that he wore with a white crew neck looked appealing on him and the jewelry decorating his body was simple yet stylish. Jigga smiled at her revealing his pretty white teeth and Bahja had to look away to keep herself from drooling at the mouth.

"But you did. I told you I'm ready for you whenever you are. What's going on with this little setup?" Jigga asked and glanced back at the shelter.

Bahja looked back at him and swallowed hard. She wanted to touch his face and see if it was as soft as it looked. Rub her hands across the beard lining his jaw and finally press her lips against his full ones. She was very attracted to him.

So much so that it frightened her.

"Could you date someone that was expecting a baby with another person?" she asked changing the subject.

Jigga sat forward and placed his elbows on his knees. It was then that Bahja was able to see the tattoos covering the side of his neck.

"I wouldn't flat out say no but I wouldn't want to be in some shit like that. I don't have any kids, but I see the bond that it places on people. That's a lifetime commitment. If you know for sure that the people don't wanna be together then you should be good but if it's any doubt, there I would say to watch out for you."

Bahja received everything he was saying, and she smiled.

"I need to get my shit together," she said with a laugh to keep from crying.

Jigga scooted her chair over to him and he placed his hand on her thigh. Bahja closed her eyes as he gently rubbed her leg back and forth.

"Sometimes you have to step out of a situation to see it for what it is. Pray on it beautiful then let him handle it. You know I'm ready to take you anywhere you wanna go but that's only if you ready. I know one thing. A nigga is supposed to do everything but make you sad. I don't know what part of the game that shit is," he said and they both laughed.

Bahja didn't either but what she did know was that sitting with Jigga outside of the shelter had been the highlight of her week.

Five

"This is different," Vashti said sitting downstairs with Bahja.

Bahja nodded thinking the same thing. They'd hosted Neveah and Emory's shower two weeks ago and was glad they'd gotten it out of the way because Neveah had woken up that morning in labor. Neveah and Emory had moved completely into their new home and was having a home birth for their girls.

Bahja and Vashti weren't aware that you could have home births for twins but apparently, you could as long as you weren't due to have a caesarian.

"Right, this nigga got food here and everything. This some Hollywood shit," Hayden, who was Emory's cousin commented sitting downstairs in the living room with everyone.

It was only a small crowd of Neveah and Emory's closest relatives. Neveah's parents were on a flight headed to Detroit while Emory's parents sat downstairs with everyone. Bahja looked at Vashti as she held her sleeping son and she smiled. Vashti's man was serving time and Bahja was proud of how well Vashti was handling things.

"How have you been?"

Vashti smiled at Bahja. Over the last few months, they'd grown really close. It had been hard at first because Vashti felt incredibly guilty for Rian attacking Bahja, but she'd learned to not place what grown people did on her. She accepted the fact that she was no longer friends with Rian and had welcomed Bahja into her life with open arms.

"I've been hanging in there. Some days are easy then some days I struggle to even get out of the bed. I miss him," Vashti replied with sadness clinging onto her every word.

Bahja rubbed her leg.

"And I'm sure he misses you as well. Try to remember the good times when that depression falls over you. You have to know that nothing lasts forever. Not even his sentence," Bahja told her.

Vashti smiled always ready to receive words of encouragement from Bahja.

"I'll do that. What about you, where is Pretty Boy?" she asked calling Micah by his street name.

Bahja shrugged. That was the million-dollar question. She seemed to see less and less of him as the days rolled by.

"I'm not Rian. I won't chase any man. Ever. If he wants to see me, he will have to show it. I won't run after him and I'll leave it at that."

Vashti laughed.

"And I would never expect for you to."

"Aye she wanna see Bahja and Vashti," Emory said walking downstairs.

Vashti passed her son to her mom and stood up with Bahja. They followed Emory upstairs and into his large master bedroom. In the center of the room was a pool. The water was being poured into it as Neveah sat on a birth ball with a frown on her face. She wore a hospital gown with her hair pulled to the top of her head. Emory gave her a quick kiss before going to the bathroom to change his clothes for the birth.

On the side of the room was four midwives assisting Neveah with the delivery. Because she was carrying twins the center, she was working with wanted extra hands available at all times. They were also checking her regularly to make sure the babies were breathing, making sure they weren't breached and also checking to make sure she was dilating how she should be.

With twin home births you always had to be extra cautious and so far, everything was going as it should be.

"Aww Neveah," Bahja said with her eyes tearing up.

Neveah smiled weakly at her friends.

"I'm so mad at you two. You bitches lied! These fucking contractions hurt," she said making every woman in the room laugh.

"You were in the room with me so don't even try it," Vashti replied walking over to Neveah.

Emory stepped out of the bathroom and went over to his lady.

"She good, she's almost there. You want some drugs?" he asked her lovingly.

Neveah whimpered as another contraction rolled around her waist like a painful tidal wave.

"No," she said quietly. "I want my mom. Emory let's just see if I can push," she said taking the pain as best as she could.

Emory caressed her neck and kissed her on the lips.

"I love you," he whispered to her while Bahja smiled on.

That was what she wanted. For a man to love her so much that everyone near them could feel and see it.

"We'll give you two some privacy," Bahja said and walked away with Vashti following her.

The two women went back downstairs and Bahja was shocked to see Micah in the living room. He looked up from his phone as she approached the sofa he was sitting on and he smiled.

"Hey baby," he said pulling her down beside him.

Bahja smiled at him and he pulled his phone back out. She tried to not pry but could see he was texting Rian.

"Bahja I heard about the blog and we are all so proud of you," Emory's mom Erykah said glancing her way.

Bahja thought of her blog and smiled. It had been doing really well and she was now getting things sent for her to review just because of the influence she had over moms on the web.

"Thank you. I can't believe it's doing so good though."

Erykah waved her off.

"We knew it would be," she replied as Bahja looked back over at Micah.

He was still texting on his phone while smiling. Bahja stood up and decided to step outside to get a breath of fresh air. Her first thought was to text Jigga, but she decided not to. He was a good ass dude and she refused to only fuck with him when she was mad. That wasn't fair to him. Instead, she went to her blog app on her phone and decided to update her followers on what was going on with her.

She titled the blog post. **Lost in translation**.

In a quest of finding myself, I found this blog. I also thought I had found new love. It wasn't easy to open my heart up to someone new. My late husband was all I had ever known but I took a chance. Things were good in the beginning but now they aren't. Something that I thought was so promising isn't anymore and I'm lost trying to figure out what's next? A good situation as somehow translated into a bad one for me. I'm not sure what to do.

Almost immediately women started to comment on the post but the answer that stood out the most was from a **King Jigga**. Under his name read the response.

Sounds to me like it's also time to find a door for that man to walk out of so that I can walk thru.

Bahja smiled to herself as she watched her women followers like his comment and even reply to him saying that he should do all that he could to make Bahja his.

"She's pushing!" Vashti said stepping outside.

Bahja put her phone away and quickly went into the house. She waited downstairs and thirty minutes later they were joined with Neveah's parents. Neveah's mom was ushered into her room while her father stayed behind with everyone else.

"This shit got me excited for my little man," Micah said to no one in particular.

Bahja found herself rolling her eyes and scooting closer towards the other side of the couch. Micah picked up on her mood and scooted over to her. He threw his arm over her shoulder and kissed her cheek.

"You been okay?" he asked her.

Bahja looked at him and smiled.

"If you have to ask me how I've been then it's a problem," she replied and stood up.

"They're both healthy and so beautiful. Eden and Ella," Neveah's mom Ladonna said walking down the stairs with happy tears covering her cheeks.

Bahja's own eyes watered and she began to cry. She remembered the nights her friend would call her in shambles behind the situation she was in with her fiancé. She remembered telling her to pray and know that things would be alright. Then, of course, like always God came through. Bahja was trying to stay hopeful and know that in the end, everything would work out for her as well. Bahja didn't want to be one of those people that preached things that she didn't believe in herself. No, she wanted to say that God had her and believe it, so she shook off the sadness consuming her body. She shook off the fear of being alone, the fear of never having that one true love and she gave it to her God.

She knew that if nobody else could help her that he could, and he was the perfect man for the job.

Six

Two Months Later.

Sorry I couldn't take that flight with you. Rian has been sick as fuck lately. I had to be there for her. Don't be mad ma.

"Thank you for coming. They are so handsome."

Bahja put her phone away choosing to not reply to Micah's text. She looked at her mom briefly before looking around the formal living room that she'd sat in millions of times before as a child. Everything was still the same. Even the décor which was kind of shocking to her but the condition of it was pristine. Not a dust particle in sight and it smelled of lilies.

Bahja's two small sons sat on the floor playing with their new toys in their matching black polos and khaki shorts. They were both handsome and replicas of their late father. Bahja could see her mother staring down at them with a big smile on her face. She wanted to still be angry with her family. A part of her never wanted to forgive them for what they'd done to her.

"We missed you and we're sorry," her mom Bina said making her look her way. She stood up and went over to Bahja. Her mom someone who never wore the same dress twice bent down in front of her and touched her legs. Bahja's mother was in great shape and looked more like her sister than her parent. "Please forgive us. Please, Bahja we want all three of you back in our lives and we're so sorry about Dave. The things we did, the things we said. My goodness, we can't take them back, but we can make up for them. Please," her mom begged now crying.

Bahja dropped her head and her father's hand was placed on the top of her shoulder.

"Please baby," he begged in his deep tone. He'd faced death, saw it coming for him, but his life had been spared. He could now see the error in their ways. He'd been ignorant and so had his family. To know he'd placed his own flesh and blood out onto the street broke his heart. They didn't deserve her forgiveness, but he prayed they still got it.

"Mama," Bahja's son Benji questioned when he saw she was crying.

Bahja smiled at him and held out her hand. Her two sons stood up and joined her on the sofa. Her mom stood and Bahja looked up at her.

"Benji and Bryan this is your grandparents," she said making both of her parents smile through teary eyes. Bahja had so many reservations. She could still remember the nights she'd slept in her car. The days she had to wash up in the public restroom because she had no home. Things of that nature placed hate in her heart towards her family. When she'd needed them most, they'd let her down. However, it was at that moment that she could hear the Lord. He told her to let go. He told her to forgive. Vengeance was his. Bahja knew that it wasn't her place to condemn them. She knew that her parents would have to answer to God for all that they had done to her. She chose to forgive and let go. She was happy. Her pain hadn't been in vain. She still had come out on the other side. She wouldn't act as if nothing ever happened, but she would be open to rebuilding a connection with them especially for the sake of her sons. As long as their intentions were good then she would consider it.

"Thank you, baby, now give them here!" her mom said excitedly and grabbed her oldest son while her father grabbed the smallest one.

Hours later Bahja sat with her father on the back terrace. Her parents had a main estate in the suburbs of Atlanta in Buckhead that sat on five acres of land. Everything from a golf course to a pool house sat on their property. Bahja and her father sipped on his favorite brandy while staring out at the vast backyard.

It was through her father that she acquired her love for liquor. They weren't addicted to it, but they often indulged in it and Bahja knew how to pick a good wine out in her sleep. Her father had a cellar filled with expensive wine.

"I've missed you so much. You're so beautiful baby and those boys of yours are something else. They're bad and they could use a spanking," he semi-joked. "But they are handsome young men. This woman that helped you, tell me about her," he said.

Bahja smiled as she thought of Neveah.

"She's the sister I've always wanted. She took me in daddy and so did her family. I will forever love them for that. The car I have belongs to her. The home we stay in is all thanks to her. Hell, even my job. I met her at the shelter."

Bahja's father frowned. His handsome face covered with confusion.

"The shelter?" He repeated quietly.

Bahja sipped her drink and glanced over at him.

"Daddy after Dave died, I had nothing. I paid for his service and a few months later I lost our home. We had no money in the bank. I never had a job besides working for the family, so I wasn't qualified for anything. It wasn't until we were out on the streets that I was able to find one. I did odd jobs and sometimes I would make enough to afford a motel and other times I didn't, so we would sleep in the car."

Bahja's father abruptly stood up. Hearing the hardships his daughter faced due to his ignorance was too much for him to handle. He stared up at the sky as pain shot through his heart. He'd failed her and his grandsons tremendously.

"I'm very sorry," he said full of remorse before walking away.

Bahja decided to give him his time and finished her drink. She attempted to call Micah as she climbed into her bed but was blindsided by a text message from Rian. Bahja's heart pounded as she stared at photos of Micah laying in Rian's bed. He was fully clothed with his hand on her round belly. Bahja sent her back a smiley face not willing to play into her game and Bahja sent her back an emoji with the woman shrugging.

You might as well just let him go. He can't seem to stay out of this bed. Are you big mad or lil mad? Let me know boo.

Bahja forwarded the photo to Micah and blocked Rian's number. She received another text only this time it was from Jigga. Bahja hadn't seen him since the shelter but had been texting him sporadically. It wasn't anything serious just friendly chatter.

Woke up with you on my mind and shit shorty. All I can think about is how sad you was looking the last time I saw you. It fucked me up to see somebody so fucking pretty look so hurt. Trust when I say that shit it's not all physical. It's something about you that just makes a nigga uneasy and shit. Like my body knows you the one and shit. Still, I won't pressure you for nothing you not ready for. You don't have to text me back I know it's been some weeks since we text and shit. Just wanted you to know that you got people pushing for you. Shit, I don't even know your full fucking name but I'm praying for you. Have a good night beautiful.

Bahja's face turned into a smile as she read over his text several times. He seemed to always know when to text or call. She licked her lips as she text him back.

Hey you. Things are better for me. I'm just getting my shit together like I told you I needed to. I didn't know you prayed for me but thank you and know after hearing that we'll be praying for each other. It's Bahja Sarkissian.

Minutes later a text from Jigga came in.

Yeah, we gotta make that Bahja Akachi.

Bahja found herself grinning at her phone before putting it away. She rested her head on her pillow as her father stepped into her room. He placed a check on her pillow then gave her a chaste kiss on her forehead and she gazed up at him.

"Nothing can fix what we've done but like your mom said before we will die trying to make things right. Even if you don't want the money take it for them. Give them the financial security that they need sweetie. I also want Neveah's parent's number, but I can get it in the morning," he said before leaving out of the bedroom.

Bahja looked at the check and her stomach knotted up. The zeroes seemed to be endless. Her father knew her well. She didn't want their money. For most of her life she'd depended on them and when she'd needed them most, they'd let her down. Now she was back on her feet without the help of them and it felt great. However, Bahja thought of her sons. For her kids, she would put her pride to the side and cash the check. She'd place the money into trust funds for them and also buy a car. Finally, she could give Neveah back her Beamer and give her the money for the house. Bahja smiled to herself and closed her eyes. She had so many things to be thankful for that Rian and her stunts were irrelevant.

"Thank you, God. Thank you," she whispered.

Seven

"I'm overly joyed right now. This blog turned into something amazing. I never knew that I could relate to so many moms but here I am. With the help of my family, I have created a magazine out of it. This magazine means so much to me. These last two months have been hectic. From finding a building and employees down to what kind of paper I will use I have been stressed. I mean in between all of that I had to still be a mom," Bahja said and everyone laughed.

Bahja grinned as her eyes scanned Vashti's salon that had been transformed into her magazine launch party. With the help of her loved ones, she'd made her dream a reality. It hurt Bahja to step away from Neveah's charity, but she had to chase her own dreams and Neveah was loving enough to understand that. Bahja now employed six people and they worked out of a small office space in downtown Detroit that she rented out. She'd been on two morning news shows and had close to a million followers online thanks to her blog. Women gravitated to her. They understood the struggle. They loved her spirit and it made her blog a hit. She was excited about the things to come and feeling overwhelmed by her sudden success.

Bahja looked around the room once more for Micah and sighed.

He was a no-show. Rian was well into her pregnancy and Bahja found herself talking to him through text more than she felt she should have been, but it was like she'd told Vashti months ago. She refused to beg for his time or attention. Instead, she'd given her all to her kids, family and new magazine. And by putting herself first she'd done something that she never thought she could do. God had truly been good to her.

"So, let's drink this wine because you all know I love a good wine and let's celebrate women. Women don't get the credit they deserve. Moms never get the accolades that they should. It's not easy and if anyone could do it then everyone would be doing it. Let's celebrate us!" Bahja said and raised her glass.

"You did good sis. We proud as fuck of you," Emory said walking over.

He was without Neveah. Their kids were doing well but with the girls being so young Neveah chose to hang back with them and Bahja completely understood. Neveah was one of her biggest supporters and she knew that her girl always had her back. Bahja also knew that being a mom was something that needed to always come first.

Bahja smiled at Emory glad to see he'd been able to show up. She gave him a hug and when he stepped to the side her breathing picked up. Jigga stood beside him holding a dozen pink roses. He wore all white and it looked amazing on his chocolate skin. Jigga's fade was freshly cut, he wore wood framed Cartier glasses with a Cartier watch. The way his eyes slid up and down Bahja made her swallow hard.

"I'm proud of you shorty," Jigga said in a sonorous voice that made her knees go weak. He pulled her into a hug and her body caved into him. Bahja hugged him tightly as his presence gave her a feeling she'd never felt before.

"Are you?" she asked quietly.

She'd been spinning him. Every now and then they would text but for the most part, she'd cut him off. Bahja had wanted to focus on her goals but also, she wasn't looking to lead him into anything until she was completely done with Micah. Something that she saw happening in the near future.

Jigga rubbed her back in slow deliberate circles. Bahja was wearing a cream pantsuit that stuck to her skin. Brought out the curves on her body and complimented her olive toned skin. Her hair was in loose flirty curls and her makeup like always was flawless.

"Hell, yeah I am. So, you ready for me or are you still trying to be lonely and shit?" he asked making her smile.

Bahja cleared her throat in an attempt to regain control of her nerves that he had going haywire.

"What the fuck is this?" Micah asked angrily as he walked up with flowers as well. His arrangement was so large he could barely hold it in one hand.

Jigga let go of Bahja and Emory shook his head. With Rian being pregnant he hadn't seen Micah in months. No one really had, so he was surprised to see him at Bahja's opening. Truthfully, he thought Micah had gone back to Rian.

"What's up nigga," Emory said trying to dap him up.

"Emory, I see what kind of fake shit you on," Micah said to him.

Emory chuckled. Micah was his people. They'd grown up together, so he wasn't looking to fight with him. He also wasn't going to take the shit talking either.

"You know a nigga ain't never been fake. I can't stop nobody from coming to some shit that's not mine," Emory replied staring Micah's way.

Micah waved him off and glared at Jigga. Jigga smirked at him and grabbed Bahja's hand.

"I can't take somebody that's not taken nigga so chill out with the looks and shit. This about Bahja ain't it?" Jigga asked pulling Bahja to his side. He'd played it safe in the beginning, but he saw how Micah was moving and felt like he was wasting Bahja's time. Jigga was ready to give her all of the love that he felt she deserved. "It's clear you don't appreciate her so why the fuck you wasting her time?" Jigga asked Micah.

Micah watched Bahja hold another man's hand and anger filled him up immediately.

"Why the fuck you speaking on some shit that don't concern you motherfucka! How many times do she gotta tell you to get the fuck out of her face?" Micah asked making a few people look their way.

"Aye now isn't the time for all of this," Emory said trying to calm Micah down.

Micah ignored Emory and shoved Jigga hard as he could making him fall back with Bahja.

"What the hell!" Vashti yelled as she watched Bahja fall on top of Jigga.

"This fuck nigga," Jigga cursed as he stood up with Bahja. Bahja was pulled to the side by Vashti as Jigga was attacked by Micah. Women screamed as Micah and Jigga tore apart Bahja's magazine launch party.

"Micah stop!" Bahja yelled in shock at what was happening.

"Nigga don't want her then gets mad when she finds somebody that do on some hoe shit," Jigga said punching Micah so hard that he momentarily closed his eyes.

Micah angrily pulled out his gun not willing to ever take an *L* fighting. Micah aimed the gun at a smirking Jigga while breathing raggedly.

"I should shoot your bitch ass," Micah told him.

Jigga smiled at him as he brushed his hand over his fade.

"Niggas that kill don't do no talking," he replied lowly noticing how frightened the people were at Bahja's party. "This shit is foul as hell nigga," he said to him.

Emory and his cousin quickly pulled Micah out of the building not wanting things to escalate and Bahja sighed with relief. Jigga fixed his clothes and turned to Bahja. She was so angry that she was crying. He shook his head hating that he'd aided in placing the tears on her face.

"Let me clean this shit up shorty," he said and grabbed the flowers off the ground.

Bahja stood back angrily as he picked up everything he and Micah had ruined. Some other men began to help him including Bahja's father. Bahja was shocked to see her father actually talking with Jigga. Her parents told her they were past the color shit but to openly see him speak with a black man warmed her heart in many ways.

"I'd love to hear more about your business," Bahja's father told Jigga as they continued straightening up the room.

Jigga patted his arm.

"You definitely will. I apologize again for all of that. This night is about your beautiful daughter," Jigga said to him.

Bahja's father glanced over at her.

"That it is," he replied, and they continued to straighten up the room.

"Let's get a drink pretty girl," Vashti said walking up.

Vashti and Bahja went to the bar and grabbed a drink. Vashti sipped on water since she was still breastfeeding while Bahja sipped on some Moscato. Bahja watched the men in attendance continue to fix up the party with Jigga leading the pack and she sighed.

"I don't know what to say," she mumbled.

Vashti shook her head.

"I feel the same way. Micah was completely out of line. I don't know every detail of your relationship with him but what he did tonight was very selfish. He hasn't even been coming around," Vashti vented.

Bahja laughed lightly.

"Exactly but chooses to pop up at my party and show his ass. He only knew about it through text. I can barely get his ass to answer the damn phone. He's too busy running up behind Rian to know what's going on with me," Bahja admitted sadly.

"I just wanted to apologize for what you all witnessed. Bahja worked hard for this to happen and I don't want my actions to fall negatively on her," Jigga said stepping into the middle of the room. His eyes connected with Bahja's and he smiled at her. "I'm sorry beautiful. Don't let nothing mess up your night," he said to her.

Everyone in the room clapped still happy to be in attendance and Bahja dropped her head while still smiling. Jigga walked up on her and pulled her to his side. He stared down at Bahja intently as she held her glass of wine.

"Come to the car and blow one with me," he said and winked at her.

Bahja nodded. She grabbed a flute on their way out of the salon and Jigga took her over to his Maserati truck. He opened the door for her, and she got in. Bahja relaxed in the seat as Jigga climbed into his truck. He leaned his seat all of the way back getting even more comfortable and pulled a blunt from his middle console. He sparked it up and his noir-like eyes glanced over at Bahja. Just being in his presence made her antsy. She could feel her leg jumping and was having a tough time looking him in the eyes.

"Why you do that?" he asked noticing she'd done that before when he'd pulled up on her at the shelter.

Bahja frowned at his question.

"What?"

Jigga tapped her shaky leg and she laughed. She swatted his hand away and he hit his blunt. Bahja watched the weed flow from between his thick lips and she swallowed hard. All she could think of is how good it would feel to have them wrap around her areolas.

"Stop that," he commented.

Bahja glanced down at her flute that was filled with wine.

"Stop what?"

Jigga placed his hand on her thigh.

"Stop staring at me like you wanna fuck me. I'm trying to be a gentleman with you. Looking at me like that gone bring the nigga up out of me. Unless that's what you want. Is it? You in need of something shorty? Just let a nigga know and I got you," he said lowly.

Bahja pressed her thighs together and swallowed her wine in one sip. She sat the glass down and Jigga sat up. He couldn't take it. Her presence was calling to him, tugging him her way and enough was enough. He'd sat back for months and went without her. Wondered what she was doing? If Micah was making her happy and clearly, he wasn't.

"Shorty that nigga isn't on his job. By now you should be married with a baby in your belly. Why the fuck you wasting your time with that clown ass nigga? I know he's not making you happy," he told her.

Bahja closed her eyes when she felt his hands caress her neck. Jigga put his blunt out and slowly unbuttoned her suit jacket. His hands roamed freely inside of it and they brushed against her white lace bra. Bahja moaned when he tweaked her nipples.

"*Jayvion*," she moaned calling him by his real name.

Jigga slid his hands up to her neck and turned her head to face him. The look in his eyes was commanding. Filled with so much lust and adoration. The stare was intense, so much so that Bahja had to break away from it. Jigga kissed the bottom of her chin before sliding his tongue around to her thick lips. The weed and liquor he had sat on his tongue still he tasted good as he brushed it against her's.

Bahja moaned and his teeth sunk into her lip.

"I wanna fuck you so bad. Stretch out that tight lil pussy and bust all in her," he said as he began to massage her breast again. The nipple stimulations quickly sent Bahja close to the edge. She'd never felt anything like it.

"Jigga," she said quietly as her skin prickled all over.

Jigga stuck his tongue in her ear as he squeezed her nipples. He'd squeeze them hard, then rub the tip and it was literally sending her over the edge.

"Jigga what? You wanna cum, let go and do it. Cum for me Bahja," he demanded and kissed her neck sensually.

Bahja's eyes closed tightly as her body gave way to his lusty demands. Her walls contracted, and she came from nipple stimulation. She struggled to catch her breath as she came down from her high.

"Did I just cum?" she asked quietly with a dry mouth.

Bahja's body was still tingling all over.

Jigga chuckled before kissing her cheek. He slid his hands into her pants and rubbed at the moist seat of her panties. Bahja's underwear were soaked. He stuffed two of his fingers into her opening after pushing her panties to the side and Bahja moaned when he moved them back and forth.

"Yeah, you did. That pussy came, and I didn't even touch her but when I put this dick up in you, she gone squirt for me. I'ma make her do magic," he promised and fingered her so good that she came for him again.

***

"I don't even know what the fuck to say."

Bahja watched her sons play on the kiddie playscape as she stood a few feet away with Micah at her side. It had been a few days after her launch party, and she was still pissed at him.

"An apology would be nice," she replied.

Micah cleared his throat as his eyes fell on Bahja. She looked beautiful as ever in her black leggings with her black off the shoulder tee and her black Balenciaga trainers on her feet. On her lips was a matte pink liquid lipstick while she wore her hair bone straight with a part down the middle.

Bahja was rare and Micah wasn't ready to ever watch her be with someone that wasn't him.

"I been fucking up. A lot. This whole thing with Rian caught a nigga off guard and shit. I could have found a way to still make you important in my life, but I can admit I slacked on that," he said after staring at her for a few minutes.

Bahja licked her lips.

"That's not enough Micah. I've been so patient with you. Gave you way too much leeway and that's my fault. All I did was aid in you hurting me. I made it easy for you to do the bullshit you're doing but no more. We don't have a title and for now, that's not changing."

Micah gritted his teeth. He looked at Bahja's sons before glancing her way.

"What the fuck are you saying exactly? You trying to cut me off for that black ass nigga? Since I'm not running up behind you, I'm useless to you now huh?" he asked angrily.

Bahja smiled at his anger. She was the type of person that listened to people when they got mad. People often showed you how they really felt when speaking in anger. She took a deep breath and exhaled. She refused to allow for Micah to make her feel guilty for wanting more.

"I'm saying that you've shown me what's important to you. You've been there for Rian every step of the way while giving me your ass to kiss. You weren't there for me when I went to see my parents or even when I started my blog. You don't know about what I have going on in my life because you haven't fucking been there. So, I'm saying to just stay where you're at. No hard feelings, it just didn't work out for us," she replied getting emotional.

Micah's jaw ticked at her words. He pulled his cap low to his head to shield his angry eyes. Instead of begging for another chance he walked away. Micah got into his Range Rover and sped out of the parking lot while blasting his music. Bahja glanced back at his departing truck before turning her attention back to her sons. She'd had such high hopes for Micah and herself, but it hadn't worked out. The whole situation had truly been a waste of her fucking time.

Bahja smiled to herself as she headed over to her sons.

"Dave I just want to be happy," she said quietly before joining her sons as they played without a care in the world at the park.

Eight

"Calm down, you look good shorty," Jigga told her.

Bahja smiled. She tugged at her red dress as they walked into the restaurant. They were immediately seated and instead of sitting across from her Jigga chose to sit beside her. While Bahja wore a red fitted dress that stopped above her knees Jigga was dressed in black jeans with a collared black Moncler polo. He was looking dapper as ever and because the two were so attractive they had everyone staring their way.

"Talk to me sexy," he said rubbing her thigh.

Two weeks. That was how long it had taken for her to see him again. The kids were spending the night with Vashti and her son, so she was free to get away.

Bahja licked her lips as her body once again felt that energy. The kind of energy that only he could provide.

"What do you wanna know?"

Jigga leaned over and kissed her neck. He couldn't help himself around her. She was so fucking beautiful and so innocent.

"Everything from the beginning. Tell me about your family," he replied.

Bahja relaxed in her seat and looked his way.

"My mom went into labor with me while on vacation in Paris. I grew up in Atlanta. My family owns jewelry stores and while working there at fifteen I met my late husband. He was so handsome," she said and smiled as she thought of Dave. "He really was. I had never met a man like him before. My family learned of our relationship and told me to leave him alone. By then I was gone off his love. He was my whole world, so I chose him. My parents eventually put me out. I married him and we, later on, had two sons together. He ended up dying in a car crash and well life got hard for me," Bahja stopped talking and Jigga pulled her to his side. Bahja was normally so calm when speaking about her past. Of course, it hurt but it had been a while since she'd teared up while talking about it. She relaxed in Jigga's arm.

The waitress came over and they quickly ordered their food. Bahja ordered a bottle of her favorite wine and Jigga kissed her neck. His presence was so calm.

Much like her's.

"I was homeless. I slept in the car with my kids, sometimes we could get a motel and sometimes we couldn't. I started staying at shelters and from there, I met Emory's wife Neveah. She was like my guardian angel. She helped me out in so many ways and from there, my journey to happiness began. We started working together and I even moved out here with her. I think that's it," Bahja said and smiled at him.

Jigga shook his head. He took off his glasses and set them on the table. He rubbed his left eye and Bahja leaned over to grab some lent off his beard. It was only a little still it had been bugging her since she'd sat down.

Jigga smirked at her. He kissed the back of her hand before putting his glasses back on. Jigga admired Bahja's beauty before he spoke again.

"And when do our story began shorty?"

Bahja broke his gaze.

"I don't know. This is still so new for me. I had my late husband. He was my first love. I never thought I would love someone the way that I loved him than the love was somehow gone. We didn't make each other feel special anymore. We were so distant. Friends instead of lovers and it hurt me. I'm the kind of girl that craves love. I need and want it because I don't feel like we were placed here not to have it. Dave didn't understand that about me then later on down the line I met Micah. He was with Emory when he came to get Neveah in Atlanta. We connected almost right away. He could relate to my struggle and he understood me. He was good with my sons and it felt right."

Jigga stroked his chin hairs with his eyes intently on her.

"And now it doesn't?" he asked.

Bahja avoided eye contact with him and nodded.

"I just wanna be happy. Is that too much to ask for?"

Jigga frowned at her.

"Hell nah, it's not. Don't ever feel bad for wanting peace in your life. If that nigga not providing that then it's time for his ass to go. I'll never kick the next nigga in his back to get to a woman so I'ma leave it at that. The choice has to be yours and no one else's. What I can say about myself is that I'ma go-getter. The power of positive thinking is a motherfucka. Whatever I see that I want, I work hard to have it and its mine. It's as simple as that and now that's you. Your fucking spirit is on a nigga. Calling my name and shit. I gotta have you and I would love and accept everything that came with you. He, not the only nigga that's good around kid's shorty," he said making her smile.

Soon the wine and food were being served and Bahja began to feel real nice along with Jigga. They exchanged flirty looks and gestures all night.

"What about you? What's your story?" Bahja asked Jigga feeling nice off the wine in her system. It had helped her relax tremendously.

Jigga glanced her way and licked his lips. Bahja was looking so delectable to him that he had to force himself to not be all up on her.

"I came from a middle-class family. I fell into the street life honestly because I had nothing to do. I wasn't into sports to the point where I wanted to play the shit, so I hung with the drug dealers. In my hood, them was the niggas you looked up to. They had all the women and the money so naturally, I wanted that as well. I ran into Emory on the block. Back when I met that nigga, we knew him as World. His ass was young but getting it and he put me on in a big way. We were running shit but eventually, that street life started getting to me. Niggas were catching cases, snitching and popping up dead. I could feel the devil on my back, so I got my ass up out of the "D". Emory was smart. He'd left the game way before I did and was always onto some new shit, but I wasn't surprised because he'd always been smart as fuck. I eventually went into business with my people and life has been good for me since then. I'm lucky to be alive honestly but all of that is behind me. I don't have no enemies or scorned exes waiting to come out of hiding and shit," he replied.

Bahja smiled at him.

"I'm happy to hear that. What happened to your cousin and Amor? Did she ever have her baby?" Bahja asked him.

Jigga swallowed some of his steak and shook his head.

"He said she still went and got that shit. He on to the next one baby. That's just Zayne plus he got a fiancé that he done been with for a minute now. Shit, he had her before I ever heard about that Amor chick. She beautiful as hell too and in college," he replied.

Bahja couldn't believe her ears. She briefly felt like reaching out to Amor but decided against it. She was still angry with how Amor had handled things at the clinic.

"Wow, I don't know what to say," she replied.

Jigga shrugged not feeling as bad about the situation as Bahja did.

"Zayne is Zayne. You'll die from stress trying to figure out why motherfuckas do the shit they do. This date is about us. Let's go hit up a club," he said pulling some money out of his wallet. He dropped some bills onto the table. Much more than what the meal was worth and they both stood up.

They exited the restaurant hand in hand. Jigga took Bahja to a low-key club that was for the older crowd. The type of people that knew how to party without causing a fight. The kind of people that enjoyed good music, good liquor and dressing nice. Jigga's older uncle had put him up on the spot and he loved it. He could relax without having to worry about shit jumping off. He found a table in the middle of the room near the dance floor for them and they ordered more drinks. Jigga liked that Bahja could handle a drink and not get pissy drunk. That was a huge turn on to him.

Bobby Womack's **If You Think Your Lonely Now** began to play and Bahja hopped up. She *fucked* with some old school music. On some days she'd sit up in the room with Neveah and they would compare playlists.

She grabbed her glass and began to sing the lyrics to the song while swaying back and forth in front of Jigga. Jigga recorded her singing for a few before rolling up a blunt. Another reason why he loved the small club. The only rule they had was no guns and because he'd been out of the streets for so long, he rarely carried a strap on him.

Unless he felt the need to.

"Honey what you know about this," an older woman sang walking over to Bahja.

Her husband sat down in Bahja's seat and looked at Jigga.

"Don't be stingy pass that shit my way," he told him and laughed.

Jigga chuckled and did as the man had asked. He watched Bahja dance and he breathed slowly. Never had he been so content with a woman without his dick being deep inside of her.

"Wait until tonight girl!" Bahja sang staring down into Jigga's eyes.

Jigga sat up and licked his lips. Bahja walked over to him and he grabbed her hips. He wanted desperately to pull her onto his lap and fuck the shit out of her.

"Your lonely days are no more," he promised looking up at her.

Bahja leaned down and kissed him tenderly on the lips. She stared into his eyes feeling her heartbeat increase.

"You promise?"

Jigga nodded immediately.

"And I don't break them shorty," he replied and kissed her again.

Nine

"This is the second magazine and we need it to be right. It has to be perfect," Bahja said and handed her son Benji his crackers. Because she missed them so much some days, she took them to work with her and today had been one of those days.

"Yum-yum," Benji said quietly and walked away in search of his brother.

Bahja smiled and when she turned around Micah stood behind her. He looked handsome as ever in his black jeans with his camo BAPE shirt. On his feet were a pair of black Maison Margella sneakers as he sported a new haircut. He gave her a small smile and held out his hand. It felt like it had been forever since she'd seen him.

"Come here ma," he said, and she took a step back.

The feeling that he'd given her when they first met was gone. She went to her office and he followed her. Micah dapped up her sons before joining her in the room. He sat across from her and took in her office space that was very kid friendly. Bahja employed nothing but moms and they often had to bring their kids to work as well so they'd created an environment that was safe for them.

"I'm proud of you. I'm happy to see you did it. I never doubted you," he told her.

Bahja smiled at him. Her cell phone began to vibrate, and Micah's eyes fell on it. Long gone was the phone he'd purchased her. Bahja was now under her own line with the same number and he had been none the wiser. She looked at him and smiled.

"Give me just a sec," she said and stood up. Bahja answered her phone as she exited her office. "*Hey,* you," she sang answering the call.

Jigga breathed into the phone.

"Tell me you're gonna bless a nigga with that pretty face today. I miss you," he said making her body tingle.

He'd been gone for two days on a business trip with his cousin.

"I miss you too. Let me call you back. Micah is here?"

"Yeah let his ass know what time it is," Micah said standing behind her.

Bahja cleared her throat.

"This nigga. Typical fuck boy shit. Lose the girl then want her back. Tell his ass it's too late now. Once you get a real nigga in your life a lame ass nigga don't even phase you. Call me when he gone baby," Jigga replied and hung up.

Bahja took Micah back into her office and they both sat down. Micah stared at her angrily as he watched her plug her phone up. Bahja was acting like shit was all good and her calm demeanor was only making him angrier.

"Yo, you really about to piss me the fuck off in here. Cause you back on money wise you think you can shit on me Bahja? Like I wasn't the same nigga doing all that I could to put a smile on your face," Micah asked angrily. He'd noticed the designer bag, the jewelry she wore and could tell that money was looking right for her again.

Bahja's head snapped back in shock. She was genuinely hurt by all that he'd said.

"Wow. That was very classless of you to say that. Please get the fuck out of my office," she told him.

Micah sighed. His anger had him saying things he didn't mean. He looked at Bahja with regretful eyes.

"I'm sorry. That was fucked up of me. I didn't mean it. I know you said you didn't want me around, but nothing has changed between us. I tried to stay away but I can't. I miss you," he said looking her way.

Bahja laughed lightly. She waved her hand around her new office.

"Micah, everything has changed. I haven't seen or spoke with you in damn near a month. We aren't even friends at this point and clearly, the feeling is mutual. Look at how you speak to me now."

Micah sighed. He sat back and cleared his throat.

"I never gave up on you ma. You was quick to walk away from me the minute shit wasn't going your way. I apologized about not being there for you before. You can't keep tossing that shit in my face. I been dealing with a lot too. My baby was born a few weeks early and not once did you call and ask me about him. He didn't do shit to you and if you got love for me then naturally you would have love for him as well. You know I fuck with your lil dudes, but did you show me that same love? Nah you been on that selfish bullshit, but I miss you and I think we can move past this. Don't keep pushing me away," he replied.

Bahja glared at Micah. He'd completely turned things around on her and she wasn't feeling it at all.

"Whatever, please just go," she pleaded with him.

Micah swallowed hard. Rian was saying all of the right things, but something kept pulling him back to Bahja. She still had a hold on him.

"I miss you. I'm not with Rian. Whenever I'm over there it's because of the baby. I apologize for not being there. I just can't let you go Bahja. Damn can't you see that I miss you?" he asked with his emotions changing the tone of his deep voice.

Bahja shook her head. In her eyes, it was too late. She wasn't looking to rehash anything that she had with Micah. Just the thought of dealing with Rian and her bullshit made Bahja cringe.

"Bahja someone is here to see you," Bahja's receptionist said peeking her head in the door.

Before she could walk away Rian was rushing into her office angrily. Micah jumped up as she tried to run over to Bahja.

Bahja's eyes darted to the other room where her sons were playing clueless to the chaos going on around them.

"I knew you would be here! The minute you heard Emory talking about her you ran over here with your punk ass!" Rian yelled and tossed her rather large cellphone at Bahja.

Bahja ducked and the phone flew through her glass wall. She'd placed the glass wall around her office, so she could see her floor space at all times.

The glass breaking caught everyone's attention. Micah held on tightly to Rian as she tried her best to fight Bahja. Never before had she felt like Micah would leave her. To think of someone else having his love literally drove her insane. She'd become someone else and although it wasn't Bahja's fault Rian couldn't stop herself from trying to take her head off.

"Bitch come here!" Rian yelled nearly foaming at the mouth.

Bahja calmly walked around her and left out of her office. Filled to the brim with anger, she rushed over to her crying sons. Rian had crossed the fucking line.

"Maxine please call the cops. I'm filing a report on that bitch so when she runs up again, I'll be able to legally defend myself," she said hugging her boys as she thought of the CCW license she'd recently acquired with the help of Jigga.

He loved guns and had her comfortable enough so that she was now shooting like a pro as well. When Bahja had disclosed to Jigga all of the things that had transpired with her and Micah he immediately knew what she needed. He'd told her that she was too beautiful to be fighting anyway. In his words, he'd said to *shoot the bitch* if she ran back up.

Bahja planned on doing just that.

Her receptionist looked at her worriedly.

"I already did! Who is this woman?" she asked.

Micah struggled with Rian inside of Bahja's office and was able to pull her out eventually. His sorrowful eyes connected with Bahja's as he walked her way with a detained Rian.

Rian had the look of the devil on her as she glared Bahja's way.

"He's mine bitch! I'll make your life a living fucking hell! You think I won't? I'll set this fucking building on fire!" Rian yelled.

Bahja let go of her sons and walked in front of Micah. Micah shook his head hating how everything was playing out.

"If he is then tell him to leave me alone. Trust I'm not the one chasing him down like you. He came looking for me, but you fucked up this time," Bahja told her.

Rian laughed like she'd told her something funny and tried to hit Bahja. She was unsuccessful but Bahja was able to slap Rian two good times before Micah shoved her back with one hand not wanting them to fight. Shock covered Bahja's face as she fell to the ground. She looked back at her sons who were watching her with teary eyes. She looked at her staff then finally at Micah. The whole scene was stupid. She didn't even want him, yet she was once again dealing with drama because of him.

Bahja jumped up and shoved Micah's arm hard.

"Leave! Get the fuck out of my life and never come back. Never, Micah!" she yelled as she started to cry.

She was hurt that she'd allowed him to pull her into his drama. Especially in front of her sons.

"I'm sorry. I really am," Micah apologized as he stared at Bahja.

Rian struggled to get free as he began to carry her away.

"Don't apologize to that bitch. You with your family let that hoe find another nigga to help her with her's," she said through gritted teeth.

Not being able to hold her tongue Bahja glared at Rian.

"Baby with a snap of a finger your man would be over here doing everything that he could for my boys plus more. That's why your confused, ignorant ass is really mad. You should be thanking me because I'm making it easy for you to have somebody that doesn't really want you. Show some fucking gratitude and get some fucking help!" Bahja said angrily.

Her assistant ran over to calm her down.

"You wish," Rian said thinking about everything Bahja had said. Still, she allowed for Micah to carry her out of the room which had been her whole point of popping up. It was to have him leave with her.

Bahja made sure they were gone before turning to her staff. She was incredibly embarrassed by everything that they had witnessed. Bahja grabbed her sons and looked at them.

"All I can say is that type of stuff will never happen again. I'm sorry," she said and swallowed hard.

Her workers nodded while some waved her off not needing an explanation. Bahja kissed her sons and took them into their play area. After making a report with the police she called Jigga who arrived at her business twenty minutes after her call to him. He showed up with his two male cousins who were beyond handsome and together the trio cleaned up her office space.

Bahja sat at her desk with her chest beating wildly. She was still so mad and contemplating calling Micah and cursing his ass out.

"Fuck them. I mean if you still hot about the shit later then I'll pull up on that nigga. I'll fuck him and her up if you want me to. But that's not you shorty. He stuck with that crazy ass bitch. Let that be his karma. Trust he gone get that shit back times ten. I already hit up my man and he coming through tomorrow to fix up your glass wall. Fuck the dumb shit and I'm happy you slapped that hoe. That shit been a long time coming," he said making Bahja smile.

Jigga went over to her and pulled her up from her chair. Bahja hugged him tightly as his arms went around her waist.

"I got you, so you can relax," he assured her and Bahja did just that. She relaxes because she could feel in her spirit that Jigga was the man for her.

Epilogue

Months later

"Slow down," she panted.

Jigga shook his head. He had that look in his eyes that told her they would be a minute. Bahja moaned as his dick did sinful things to her.

Things that had her wanting to do nothing but lay in a bed with him all day.

"We need to go," she said weakly.

Jigga nodded. He grabbed her hips and pulled her slightly up. He'd shown her that he could make love to her mentally and physically. Jigga had mastered making her cum and knew just how to hit it.

"Baby, fuck! God.... slow down," Bahja whimpered as he repeatedly pounded against her spot. Her legs began to tremble and Jigga went deeper. He shifted to the left just a little and like a faucet, Bahja leaked for him.

"Shittt!" she yelled as her eyes ventured to the back of her head.

Jigga felt her wetness shooting against him and it made him bust prematurely. He leaned down and kissed Bahja passionately as they both climaxed together.

"Look at you cumming all over me. Let's go get married," he whispered against her lips.

Bahja shook her head to clear the intimate moment she'd had earlier from her mind.

"A lot can happen in a year. Children can be born, and weddings can happen," Bahja said thinking of Neveah who'd married the love of her life Emory in an intimate ceremony. "Things that make you cherish being alive. It's little pretty moments like that I live for. I'm tired. This baby just got in me and already it's giving me the blues, but I had to thank everyone for coming to our reception. We didn't want anything to be over the top plus we all promised Gunner that we would keep our nuptials simple so that he could come home and do it big." Bahja stopped talking and looked at Jigga. He was an amazing man.

He was everything she'd always wanted. He was made just for her and that's why he was now her husband.

"This man has been my rainbow. The light at the end of my storm. I'm emotional you guys for several reasons so please excuse me if I cry. For one I can't drink, and the other reason is because I am unbelievably happy. Like so happy I wanna shout it out to the world. He loves me in ways that I had never felt before. He loves me how I *should* be loved, and I promise it's getting returned. Tonight, we celebrate us and I'm appreciative of the people that wanted to witness that. Thank you," Bahja said and sat down.

Jigga pulled her to his side and rubbed her flat belly as he looked at her intently.

"I love you. The minute you feel I don't we gone have a problem."

Bahja laughed. He always said things of that nature and she believed him. The thing was she felt the exact same way. She grabbed his face and kissed his lips while gazing into his eyes.

"Same here. You stop loving me and we're making the First 48 baby," she jabbed back making him chuckle.

In the past, Micah had reached out to her several times before finally giving up. Bahja hadn't wanted to rush things with Jigga but she'd listened to her heart. He loved her and her sons. They were a team and with him things were real. She didn't care if people felt they were moving too fast. It worked for them and they didn't give a fuck about the people that had something to say about it.

Micah was now with Rian and Bahja felt nothing behind that news. She didn't hate Micah she simply wished she'd listened to her first mind when it said to cut him off. She could have saved herself a lot of time. Instead, she was trying to make something work with someone that had too much on his plate.

Jigga kissed Bahja's neck pulling her out of her thoughts and she smiled at him.

"I love you shorty, tell your man you love him back, so we can finish this dinner. I'm ready to get your ass alone again," he said with a smile.

Bahja blushed and Jigga stuck his tongue out to her. Seductively she sucked on it until she felt her panties go moist. Bahja laughed and buried her face into Jigga's neck. Jigga was nasty but she liked it. That had been how she'd gotten pregnant.

"I love you so much baby, but you already know that. You made it easy for me to love again," she whispered.

Also by Dominique Thomas

the heartbreak shorts
Can I Love Again

Standalone
Coming Up Short